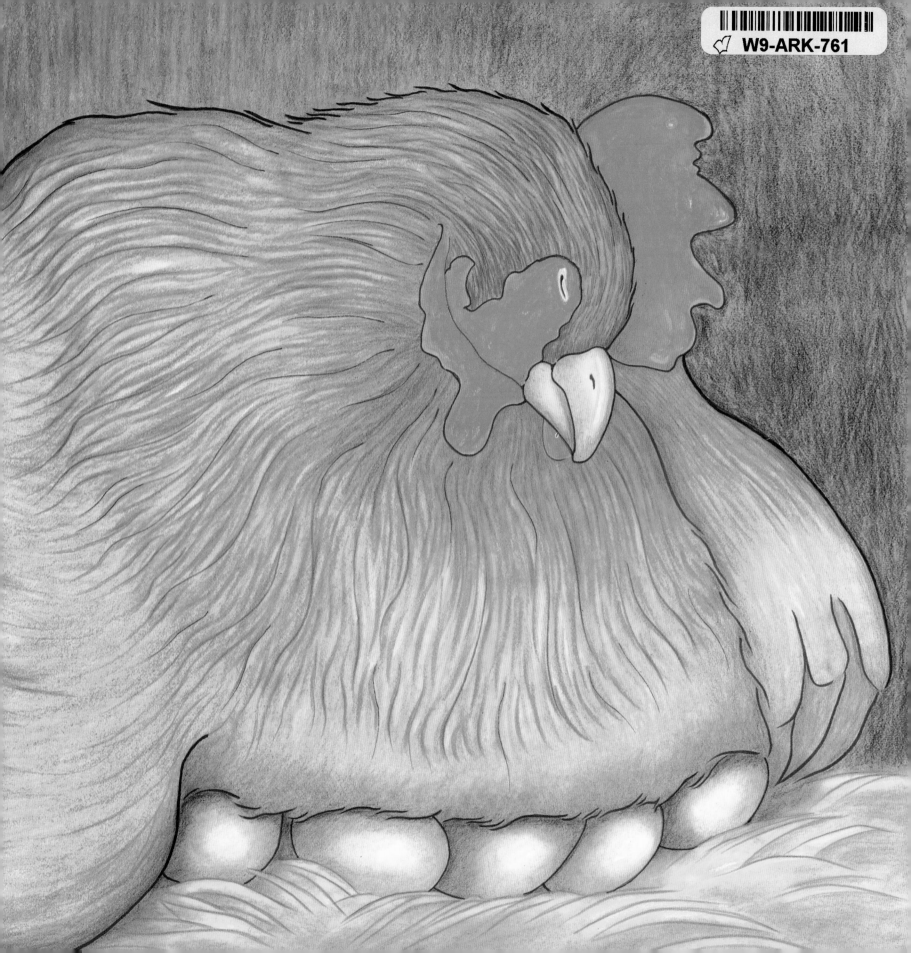

For my little chick, Cristina

Five Little Chicks

Nancy Tafuri

Simon & Schuster Books for Young Readers
New York   London   Toronto   Sydney

Once there were

peep

five little chicks!

peep

Said the first little chick,
"Peep! What can I eat?"
And with a little squirm,
spied a fat, wiggly worm.

Said the second little chick,
"Peep! What can we eat?"
And with a little shrug,
found a spotted, crawly bug.

peep

peep

Said the third little chick,
"Peep! What can we eat?"
And with a little sigh,
saw a fuzzy butterfly.

Said the fourth little chick,
"Peep! What can we eat?"
And with a little worry,
spotted a plump, red strawberry.

Said the fifth little chick,
"Peep! What can we eat?"
And with a little pout,
saw a long, shiny trout.

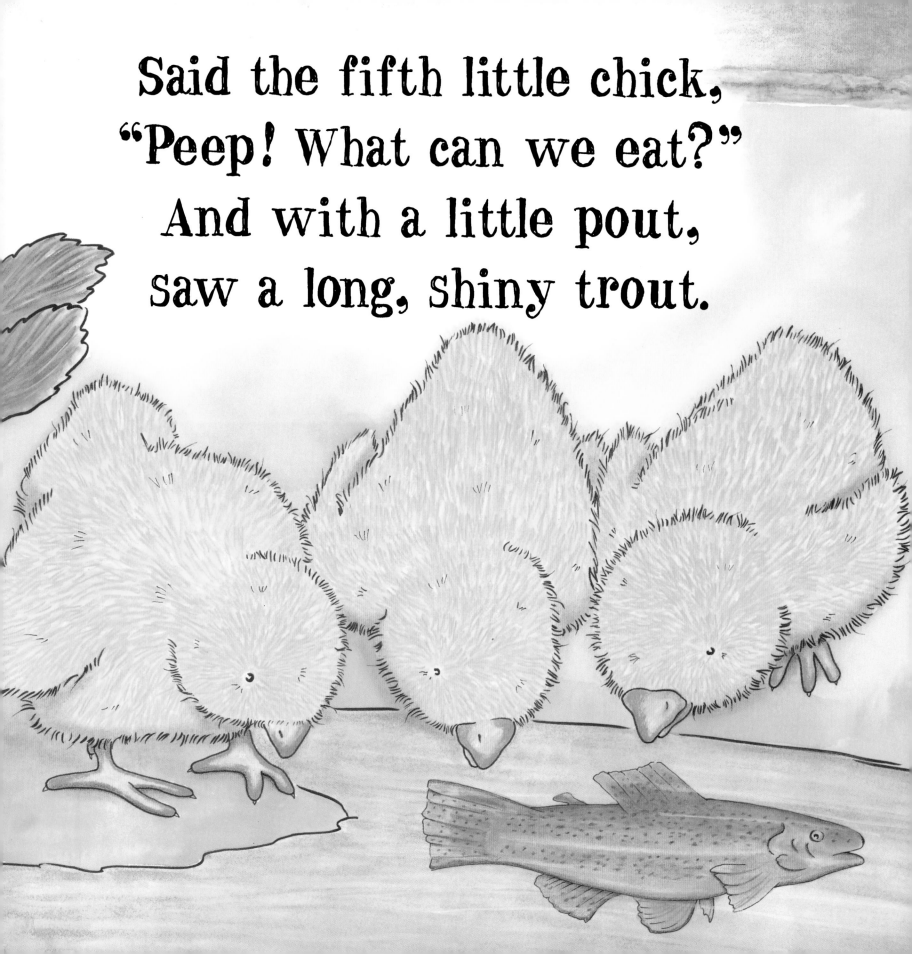

peep

cluck
cluck

But wise Mama Hen
knew just what to do.
"Let's run to the patch . . .

and scratch!"

So all five chicks went

scratch,

scratch,

scratch,

And pecked with their mama

all day in the corn patch!

Until wise Mama Hen said,
"Let's not make a peep!
It's time to snuggle and
cuddle and sleep."

cluck
cluck

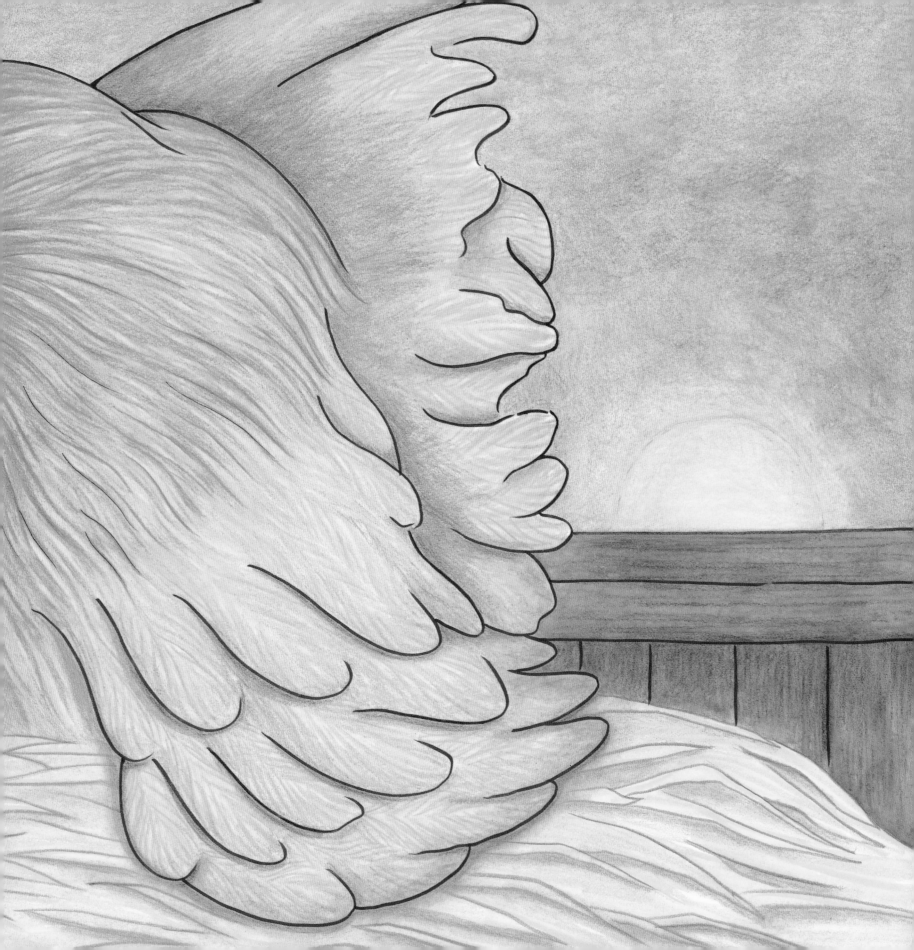

"Good night,
my five little sweets.
Sleep, sleep."